✳ ✳ ✳

ISBN: 978-0-7364-2894-1
randomhouse.com/kids
Printed in the United States of America
10 9 8 7 6 5 4 3

DISNEY FAIRIES

SECRET of the WINGS

The Junior Novelization

Adapted by Sarah Nathan

Random House 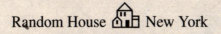 New York

One

High up in the evening sky, the Second Star to the Right glows brightly. If you follow that star, you'll find the magical island of Never Land. It is a wonderful place, filled with tall mountains, flowing rivers, and deep forests. And in the very heart of Never Land is Pixie Hollow, the home of all the fairies.

Pixie Hollow is very different from the mainland, where the humans live. For one thing, all four seasons occur in Pixie Hollow at the same time. There's Spring Valley, where flowers always bloom. And Summer Glade, where it's warm and sunny every day. In the Autumn Forest, leaves turn colorful shades of red, gold, and orange. And just over the border, where no warm-weather fairy is permitted to go, are the Winter Woods. Shimmering white snow blankets the world there, and ice-topped mountain peaks overlook frozen valleys, brooks, and streams. Warm-weather fairies live on one side of the border, and cold-weather fairies stay on the other. A winter fairy cannot survive the heat of spring or summer. And the icy temperatures of the Winter Woods would freeze a warm-weather fairy's wings. So the fairies stay in their seasons and keep busy with their work. They know that the rules are there to protect them, and that crossing the border can be very dangerous.

One bright and busy morning in the Autumn Forest, Silvermist, a water-talent fairy, flew along the river. A handful of dragonflies buzzed around her. They were collecting dewdrops to place on spiderwebs. Not far away, a garden fairy named Rosetta was coaxing flowers to bloom.

Vidia, a fast-flying fairy, zipped overhead. The wind from her wings pushed the autumn leaves through the air. Each fairy had a job to do, and they were all happily finishing their morning tasks. But perhaps no fairies were quite as busy as the tinkers. They were expecting a very special arrival in Tinkers' Nook!

"Look sharp, everyone!" Fairy Mary, the head of the tinker fairies, called. "The snowy owls will soon be arriving to take the snowflake baskets to the Winter Woods." She looked around and noticed that a tinker fairy named Lucinda was not focused on her job. "Lucinda, stop noodling and start tinkering!" she scolded. Then she flew off to check on the basket production.

Nearby, a friendly gray mouse named Cheese was struggling with his wagon. It was filled with bundles of reeds, and it was a bit too heavy for him to pull. Suddenly, a lasso appeared out of nowhere and picked up a bundle of reeds from the cart, making the load lighter. Cheese looked up and saw that his friend Tinker Bell was holding on to a pole attached to the rope. Leave it to Tinker Bell to create an invention like a pole with a swinging lasso to help a friend in need!

"Is that the last load?" Tinker Bell asked the mouse with a satisfied smile.

Cheese replied with a happy squeak to say "Yes!"

Tinker Bell waved and flew off to help her other friends.

"Morning, Clank! Morning, Bobble!" she called when she reached the basket depot. The two tinkers were busy weaving long reeds into sturdy baskets. She placed the new bundle on a pile in front of them. "That should be enough to finish the snowflake baskets," she said.

Bobble looked up. His thick dewdrop goggles made his eyes seem enormous. "Aye, that'll do her," he agreed.

"Thanks," Clank added. He smiled at Tinker Bell and didn't watch what he was doing. He accidentally wove the reeds right over Bobble's hands!

"Clanky!" Bobble complained, trying to free himself.

"Sorry," Clank apologized. Tinker Bell giggled. Her friends were always getting into funny mishaps like this. Granted, Tinker Bell had a way of getting into tricky situations herself. One time, she had almost ruined the preparations for bringing spring to the mainland. And just this past summer, she had accidentally been captured by a little girl in the human world. But each time, her friends had helped her find a way to fix the problem. And right now, Tinker Bell couldn't get into any trouble at all because she was doing her very favorite thing: tinkering!

She looked around at the towering piles of baskets that were ready to be collected by the snowy owls. "I can't believe we make the baskets but don't get to take them to the winter fairies," she said. "I mean, wouldn't you want to go into the Winter Woods?"

Both Clank and Bobble stopped their work and stared

at Tinker Bell in disbelief. "We wouldn't last a day in that cold," Bobble said, shivering. "You'd get frostbite on your fingers, your face would freeze, and . . . Tell her, Clank."

Clank nodded in agreement. "You'd get pounced on by a glacier!" he finished.

Bobble raised an eyebrow, and Tink looked at both of them in confusion.

"They're known for their stealth," Clank insisted.

Bobble turned to Tink. "He's never actually seen one," he said.

"You never do," Clank said ominously. "Until it's too late."

Suddenly, a loud horn sounded. All the tinker fairies looked up to see a flock of snowy owls rapidly approaching.

"Places, everyone!" Fairy Mary called.

Instantly, the fairies began operating a large pulley that hauled the freshly woven baskets up to a delivery tower.

One by one, each of the snowy owls dove down and

snatched a basket in its talons. Then, together, the flock soared back into the sky. Tinker Bell watched, her eyes wide with excitement. The large white birds were so graceful and strong!

A young owl approached the basket pickup. He swooped down to grab one of the baskets. But it was a little too heavy for him. He wobbled as he lifted back into the air.

"Oh, newcomer," Fairy Mary said knowingly.

After struggling for a moment, the young owl gained speed and flew to join his brothers. Before the flock left, one of the owls dropped a note made of ice down to Fairy Mary. It floated softly on a frozen parachute. The second it touched Fairy Mary's hands, the ice began to melt. So she had to read it quickly.

"The final shipment order," Fairy Mary said. "Goodness! They need twenty more baskets for tomorrow's pickup!"

But Tinker Bell was only half listening. She couldn't help watching as the owls headed for the horizon. They were flying back to the cold mountain range of the mysterious Winter Woods.

"There's a whole other world over there," Tinker Bell said wistfully to Clank and Bobble. She couldn't explain it, but Tink felt drawn to the Winter Woods. It was as if there were a secret buried there, deep in the snow, just waiting to be discovered.

Two

"Look out!" a voice called.

Tinker Bell, Clank, and Bobble all turned at the same time. Fawn, an animal fairy, was chasing a bunny as it scampered through the basket depot.

"Runaway bunny!" Fawn exclaimed.

The rabbit bounded through the workshop, scattering reeds and supplies everywhere. Baskets went flying through the air!

In a flash, Tinker Bell zipped over and used her special lasso to grab hold of the renegade bunny.

"Gotcha!" Tinker Bell declared proudly. The bunny wriggled its nose. It was not happy to have been caught.

"Thanks, Tink," Fawn panted, flying up next to her.

"No problem," Tink replied.

Fawn reached over and tried to calm the bunny down. "Come on, little guy," she said. "It's still a long way to the Winter Woods."

Tinker Bell's eyes lit up. "Oh! You're taking the animals today?" she asked.

Fawn sighed. "Trying to," she said. "It's time for them to cross the border. But this little guy's a handful."

Tink fluttered her wings excitedly. This was her chance to see the Winter Woods up close! "Hey, uh . . . how about if I help?" she asked, her eyes shining.

A short while later, Tinker Bell and Fawn were racing through the Autumn Forest with the animals. Fawn was guiding several weasels, a few bunnies, and a marmot. Tink was trying to steer the youngest bunny by using her tinkered lasso as a leash. But the rabbit was so fast that she kept bouncing along behind it instead.

"Slow down!" Tinker Bell yelled. "Whoa!"

Fawn looked over her shoulder and grinned. "Need some help?" she asked.

"Nope," Tinker Bell said. "Doing fine!"

Finally, they reached the border between the Autumn Forest and the Winter Woods. Tinker Bell was just settling her bunny down when she looked up and saw the border for the first time. She gasped. It was amazing! A wide chasm separated the two seasons, and a thin curtain of soft, shimmering snow fell down the center, marking the divide. Down at the bottom of the trench, a rushing stream babbled on the autumn side. But once it reached the winter side, the water froze solid. A long bridge connected the two seasons. Half of it was a log, and the other half was ice.

"Wow," Tinker Bell whispered.

The bunny beside her trembled nervously.

"Awww," Fawn said, patting the bunny's side. "Don't be scared, little fellow. We'll let the weasels go first."

Fawn guided the weasels to the bridge as Tinker Bell watched curiously.

"So how far do we take the animals in?" Tink asked.

"Uh, Tink, we don't cross the border," Fawn replied. "We just help the animals."

Tinker Bell raised her eyebrows in disbelief. "But I thought animal fairies got to cross with the animals?"

Fawn shook her head. "Tink, it's freezing over there," she explained. "Besides, no warm fairies are allowed in the Winter Woods. Just like winter fairies aren't allowed over here."

Tinker Bell looked at the beautiful falling snow. "Who made up that rule?" she asked, disappointed.

"I think it was the Lord of Winter," Fawn replied. Then she turned back to the weasels. "All right, guys," she said encouragingly. "You ready?"

The weasels chattered their agreement. Then they skipped up the log. One at a time, they leapt over into winter. As they crossed the border, each of the weasels' coats magically turned from brown to white!

"Wow!" Tinker Bell exclaimed.

Fawn smiled. "Pretty great, huh? They get their winter coats to protect them from the cold."

Next, three baby bunnies hopped up to the bridge. They bounded over the border, and their fur also quickly transformed from brown into brilliant white.

Fawn flew over to Tinker Bell's bunny. "Go on, now," she said gently. "Follow your brothers."

The bunny's ears perked up. He didn't seem as afraid now that the other animals had all crossed. He hopped to the edge of the bridge and stretched out his ears until they just reached across the border. The tips turned white! Then he spun around and wiggled his tail on the winter side. It turned white, too!

Tinker Bell giggled. "Bye-bye!" she called as the bunny finally hopped all the way into winter. Tink fluttered closer to the curtain of falling snow. What was it like over there? she wondered. Had any fairy ever tried to cross?

Behind her, Fawn was wrestling with a very sleepy marmot. It was his turn to go. But he was already starting to hibernate, right there in the Autumn Forest.

"Oh, no," Fawn groaned when the marmot let out a loud snore. "No hibernating yet. You do that in winter!" She nudged him toward the log bridge. "Come on. Wake up!"

Meanwhile, Tinker Bell was scanning the crisp, white snow that stretched far out on the other side of the border. It shimmered and sparkled in the winter sunlight. Tinker Bell couldn't help it. She just had to see what winter was like!

Remembering what the bunny had done, she reached her hand over the border. Then she quickly drew it back. Nothing! She glanced over her shoulder to see if Fawn was watching. But her friend was distracted by the sleepy marmot. Now was Tinker Bell's chance!

Gaining confidence, Tink leaned over the border and stuck her nose across. "Oooh," she said, feeling the tingle of cold air. Her nose was chilly. But it didn't hurt at all.

With a deep breath, Tinker Bell jumped over the border! Instantly, the frosty air surrounded her. Tink shivered. But the snow was magnificent! Tiny flakes swirled everywhere, glistening like pixie dust. Tink opened her mouth and let one land right on her tongue. It was deliciously cold.

Suddenly, Tinker Bell felt a very strange sensation in her wings. She turned around and gasped. Her wings were sparkling! They shimmered with a brilliant burst of colorful light she had never seen before. She could even see all their delicate patterns illuminated. What was causing them to shine so brightly?

As if from far away, Tink heard a baby's laugh. It was very soft. But the sound echoed in her ears.

"Tink?" Fawn's call was distant and faint.

Tinker Bell's wings stopped sparkling.

"Tinker Bell!" Fawn cried.

"Wha—?" Before Tink knew what was happening, a lasso sailed over her head and tightened around her waist.

"Aaagh!" she yelled as Fawn yanked her back past the border into autumn.

"Tink!" Fawn exclaimed. "I told you we're not allowed to cross." She brushed her hand against her friend's wing. "Your wings!" she gasped.

Tinker Bell's eyes shone. "I know!" she cried. "They were sparkling!"

"They're freezing," Fawn said. "We'd better get you to a healing-talent fairy."

Tinker Bell tried to protest. But Fawn dragged her away from the border. "Come on!" she cried. Fawn knew that Tinker Bell's wings were in great danger. They had to get help—and fast!

Three

Nestled among the roots of the Pixie Dust Tree was the fairy hospital. There were many patients inside waiting to be seen by healing talents. But some were not so patient.

"Um, how much longer?" a fairy covered in rainbow-colored stripes asked anxiously.

The receptionist at the front desk looked up. "I told you, a rainbow collision is not an emergency," she said.

The fairy scratched his arm. "But the purple is starting to itch," he complained.

The receptionist shook her head. "Take a seat."

Just then, Silvermist, Iridessa, and Rosetta flew in. They had heard the news about Tinker Bell and were very concerned about their friend.

"Hurry, girls!" Rosetta called over her shoulder as she shot through the waiting room.

"Faster!" Silvermist cried.

"What if we're too late?" Iridessa asked.

"Ahem." The receptionist cleared her throat as the fairies sailed right by her check-in desk. There was nothing that annoyed the receptionist more than fairies not following proper procedure.

The three friends stopped midflight. They hadn't even noticed the receptionist.

"Oh, sorry," Iridessa said. "Do you know where—"

"Patient's name?" the receptionist interrupted.

"Tinker Bell," Rosetta and Silvermist said together.

"Oh, yes." The receptionist nodded. "The border crosser. She's . . ."

"Frozen solid?" Iridessa cried.

The receptionist sighed. "Room Two."

"Thank you," Silvermist called as she and her friends

raced off. The trio zipped up and down the hallways of the fairy hospital, looking for the right room.

"Come on, girls, hurry," Rosetta said urgently.

A moment later, they all piled into an examining room. Tinker Bell was sitting on a table with a firefly lamp shining down on her wings. A healing-talent fairy was studying her wings closely while Fawn stood off to the side.

"We got here as quick as we could," Rosetta said.

"We did have to stop at reception," Silvermist explained.

"Did you really cross?" Iridessa asked.

Tinker Bell was touched that her friends had dropped everything to come see her. She couldn't wait to tell them how her wings had sparkled!

But she didn't get the chance to answer, because the healing fairy cut off their chatter. "Shhhh," the fairy scolded them.

The three friends nodded and grew quiet. Still, Iridessa couldn't stand not knowing what had happened. She leaned in close to Tinker Bell. "Well, did you?" she whispered loudly.

"Shhh!" the healing fairy snapped. She made the light brighter and moved her magnifying glass over Tinker Bell's wings.

Just then, Vidia sped into the room. When she saw Tinker Bell's wings magnified under the glass, she gasped. "Whoa," she said.

Tink's other friends shot her a look. "Shhh!" they all hushed Vidia together.

Finally, the healing fairy took a step back. "Okay," she said to Tinker Bell. "You're all warmed up. Let's test your wings."

Tinker Bell sat up a little straighter.

"Open," the healing fairy instructed. "Close."

Tinker Bell did as she was told.

"Try a little flap," the healing fairy said.

Tinker Bell quickly flapped her wings.

"Can you give me a flitter?"

Tinker Bell took a deep breath and flittered her wings. They felt perfectly normal.

The healing fairy looked pleased. "Well, I don't see anything unusual. Your wings appear to be fine."

Tinker Bell's friends sighed in relief.

"But what about the sparkling?" Tink asked.

"Hmm," the healing fairy said, gathering her things to see the next patient. "Well, it must have been the light reflecting off the snow."

"But . . . ," Tinker Bell protested.

The healing fairy gave her a stern look. "You should have never crossed the border," she scolded her. "Winter is too cold for our warm fairy wings. Now, to be safe, I want you to take two sunflower seeds and come back if there is any problem."

Together, Tink's friends led her out of the fairy hospital. They were all relieved that Tinker Bell was okay.

"We were worried," Silvermist said.

"You are so lucky nothing happened to your wings," Fawn added.

"Can you imagine?" Rosetta shook her head.

Tinker Bell looked around at her friends. "But something did happen," she tried to explain. "They sparkled!"

Iridessa patted her on the shoulder. "You heard the healing fairy. It was just the light reflecting off the snow."

"No, it wasn't!" Tinker Bell insisted. "They actually lit up! It was brighter than a thousand fireflies." She turned to Fawn. "You saw it, didn't you?" she asked.

Fawn looked down at her feet. "No . . . ," she said finally.

Tink's shoulders slumped. "You don't believe me?" She sighed when her friends shook their heads. "Look, you guys. It happened. It felt like . . . like . . ."

"Like what?" Silvermist asked.

Tinker Bell gazed off into the distance. "Like the Winter Woods was calling me," she whispered.

Her friends all looked at one another anxiously. Now Tinker Bell was really acting crazy!

"Uh-huh," Rosetta said slowly. Then she whispered to the others, "Get the doctor!"

Tink sighed. It didn't matter what the healing fairy had said. She knew her wings *had* sparkled. She wished her friends believed her. And more than anything, she wanted to know what the sparkling had meant.

Four

Later that day, Tink flew off to the Book Nook. She had a feeling that she might be able to find the answer to her question there.

The library was a cozy little building tucked inside a hollow tree. As she entered, Tink passed by four fuzzy bookworms carrying stacks of books to reshelve.

Soon she found herself flittering down a long row of shelves crammed with dusty books. Under her breath, she read the titles aloud. *"101 Uses for Pixie Dust. Beauty and the Bees."* She shook her head. "There's got to be a wing book here somewhere," she mumbled. *"How to Avoid Hawks. Rules for Rainbow Riding.* No . . . not that." Her finger trailed along the row of spines as she scanned each title, looking for the right one.

Suddenly, a tattered-looking book caught her eye. She opened it and found that the pages had been chewed through. "Hey!" she exclaimed, poking her finger through the hole in the page. "Someone's been eating the books!"

Nearby, a chubby bookworm looked up guiltily. A half-eaten page was sticking out of his mouth. He quickly gulped down the paper and inched away.

"Ugh," Tinker Bell said, rolling her eyes.

She kept searching until, finally, she struck gold.

"*Wingology*!" she exclaimed. Tink reached for the book. It was shaped like fairy wings. But before she could grab it, the book magically took flight! Tinker Bell chased after it, causing a commotion throughout the library. The book slammed into stacks and shelves, knocking other books all over the floor. Finally, Tink pinned it down on one of the sturdy mushroom-cap tables. "Gotcha!" she cried.

A fairy wearing thick glasses at the next table

cleared his throat. He seemed annoyed.

"Oh, sorry," Tink apologized. Quietly, she began to flip through the pages. After a moment, she found just what she was looking for. "Sparkling! I knew it!" she cried.

She raised her hands triumphantly. The book took advantage of her distraction and tried to fly off once more. Tink slammed it back down.

Again, the fairy with glasses shot Tink a warning look.

"Sorry!" she whispered. Then she turned back to the book's explanation of sparkling wings. "Oh, no!" she exclaimed. The page that had the answer to Tinker Bell's question was chewed up. The bookworm must have gotten to it first. Tinker Bell glared at the chubby worm.

"Thanks a lot," she grumbled.

The bookworm gave her another guilty look. He had just started munching on a tasty paper snack. He slid away, taking the snack with him.

Tinker Bell sighed and tried to make sense of the words

that were left on the page. " 'Sparkling wings,' " she read, " 'when a . . . most incredible . . . that the sparkle . . . there were two.' " Tinker Bell blew her bangs out of her face as she tried to figure out what the words meant. *Two of* what? she thought. *Two wings? Two feet?*

Frustrated, she moved over to where the fairy with glasses was reading. "Pssst," she whispered. "Do you know anything about sparkling wings?"

The fairy looked up from his book. "No," he replied. "The bookworm ate that page."

"Yeah, I know." Tinker Bell sighed.

"But the Keeper does," the fairy said.

"The Keeper?" Tinker Bell asked. "Who's the Keeper?"

The fairy pushed his glasses up higher on his nose and pointed to the author's name on the front cover of the book. In small letters, it read, BY THE KEEPER.

"He writes the books," the fairy told her. "He is the keeper of all fairy knowledge."

"That's perfect!" Tinker Bell exclaimed. "Is he here? I have to talk to him."

The fairy chuckled. "I would give anything to talk to him. But you can't. He's a winter fairy. In order to talk to him, you have to go to the Winter Woods."

When Tinker Bell looked at him expectantly, the fairy continued. "And that's impossible. Your wings will freeze and . . ." He snapped a pencil he was holding in half. "Chapter sixteen," he said, nodding to the book.

"The Winter Woods," Tinker Bell whispered. She quickly thanked the fairy and started to fly home.

I have to see the Keeper! she thought eagerly. *Somehow, there has to be a way to cross the border safely. He's the only one who can tell me why my wings sparkled!*

Five

A short while later, Tinker Bell was hard at work in her teapot home. Using thorn scissors, she snipped a thick green leaf into pieces. Nearby, two bugs turned a spinning wheel to make thread. Tink carefully stitched the pieces of the leaf together to make a warm winter coat. Then she started to make snow boots. She hammered and cobbled until they were just right. She even added her signature pom-poms to the toes. When she was done, she tucked fuzzy earmuffs and woolly gloves into her satchel, along with the *Wingology* book. She looked at herself in the mirror.

Not bad! she thought. She was ready for winter!

Smiling, she turned to fly off on her adventure . . . and fell flat on her face!

"Agh!" Tinker Bell grunted. She'd forgotten that with her warm coat on, she couldn't flap her wings.

Luckily, with the plan she had in mind to get to the Winter Woods, something *else* would be doing the flying for her!

Outside Tinkers' Nook, Tinker Bell cautiously peeked out from behind a bunch of leaves. She saw Fairy Mary and the other fairies hard at work in the basket depot. Slipping her hood over her head, Tinker Bell quietly tiptoed into the workshop.

"Stand by with the pulley," Fairy Mary was instructing the tinkers in a loud voice. "It's this season's final pickup, so let's make it our best."

Tink hid behind a large bin and spied on her friends Clank and Bobble. They were testing out the basket they had just made.

"Okay, Clanky!" Bobble shouted from inside the basket.

Clank pulled down on a large lever, and the bottom of the basket opened up. Bobble fell through it and onto the ground with a loud *thump!*

"Snowflake release system working!" Clank declared. He smiled proudly

Bobble rubbed his head. "Maybe *you* should be the test snowflake for a while," he mumbled.

Without a sound, Tink pulled a small thorn grappling hook attached to a rope out of her satchel. Quickly, she tossed the hook toward the top of the basket. It caught hold. Pleased with herself, Tink began to climb up and into the basket. She was so close to getting a ride to the Winter Woods!

"Tink?" Clank suddenly called.

Uh-oh, Tinker Bell thought. She'd been caught!

"We already checked that basket," Bobble called up, confused. He thought Tinker Bell was helping them prepare for the final pickup.

"R-right, uh . . . ," Tinker Bell stammered as she slowly lowered herself back to the ground. She had to think fast.

Clank looked Tink up and down curiously. "Why are you dressed all cozy?"

Tinker Bell sighed. It was no use trying to lie to her friends. "I'm going to the Winter Woods," she said.

Clank and Bobble gasped.

"The Winter Woods!" Bobble cried.

"Shhh!" Tinker Bell looked around for Fairy Mary. Thankfully, the head tinker fairy was busy on the other side of the factory, counting the last batch of baskets.

"The Winter Woods?" Bobble whispered.

Tinker Bell was about to explain when suddenly a loud horn sounded.

"Places, everyone!" Fairy Mary called.

"The snowy owls!" Tinker Bell gasped, her heart beating fast. "They're here!"

"Start the pulley!" Fairy Mary ordered.

The baskets that the tinker fairies had been making all day started to move along the rope up to the delivery tower. Tinker Bell didn't have time to think. It was now or never.

"Bye," she whispered to Clank and Bobble. Before they could stop her, Tink hoisted herself into a moving basket and began rising into the air.

"Tink, wait!" Clank cried, sounding worried. He looked over at Bobble, and the two friends flew after her.

The pulley was carrying baskets up to meet the snowy owls as they swooped down. Tinker Bell's basket was nearing the top.

"You can't cross the border, Miss Bell," Bobble whispered urgently over the rim. "Your wings—"

"Don't worry," Tinker Bell said. "They're in my coat."

"Does this have to do with the sparkling?" Clank asked.

"Yes," Tink answered. "And there's somebody in winter who can tell me what it means."

"Clank? Bobble?" Fairy Mary's voice echoed from

down below. "Is there something wrong with that basket?"

"Wh-what? Oh, um . . . ," Bobble stammered. He shot Tink a nervous glance. She looked at him pleadingly. They couldn't give her away now!

"Tink," Bobble begged one last time.

"I just have to do this," Tinker Bell whispered.

Bobble turned back to Fairy Mary. "Uh, no. Everything is, uh, fine," he said.

"We're just sad to see it go," Clank added. He patted the side of the basket. "Pretty basket."

Fairy Mary rolled her eyes and let out a heavy sigh. "Oh, honestly!" she said. "Let it go!"

Clank and Bobble released their hold on the basket, and one by one the snowy owls swooped down to collect the deliveries. Tinker Bell peeked over the edge. Her basket was next for pickup!

Just then, the young owl from the previous day came into view. He was assigned to collect Tinker Bell's basket.

"Oh, that's the new one," Fairy Mary said to Clank and Bobble.

Tink's friends gulped. A new owl wouldn't be as steady when picking up a heavy basket as the other, more experienced owls. They hoped the bird wouldn't drop Tinker Bell!

A moment later, the young owl flew past and grabbed the handles of Tinker Bell's basket. He wobbled a little. Then he flapped his wings hard, trying to keep up with his brothers.

Tinker Bell smiled. They were on their way . . .

. . . and heading straight for a wall! Panicking, Tinker Bell crouched against the side of the basket and braced for impact. But at the last second, the determined little owl gained enough momentum to lift the basket up and over the wall. They just missed it.

Back on the ground, Clank and Bobble let out a sigh of relief. That was close!

Tinker Bell sneaked a look back at her friends one last time, then she quickly ducked down.

"Excellent work, everyone," Fairy Mary praised the tinkers in the depot. "They're off to the cold of winter." She looked around. "Well, that's that until next year."

As Fairy Mary left, Clank and Bobble continued watching Tinker Bell's basket disappear over the horizon.

"Stay warm, Miss Bell," Bobble whispered softly.

Six

Inside the basket, Tinker Bell was nervous and excited. There was no turning back now. She was going to the Winter Woods!

Peering over the edge, she saw the border between autumn and winter rapidly approaching. It grew closer, and closer, and then . . .

Fwoom!

The moment they crossed over, a burst of cold air hit Tinker Bell hard. She shivered and opened her eyes. She was in winter!

The snowy owl flew on at top speed. Tinker Bell held tight and watched as a world of white whizzed past her. Winter was incredible! They dipped under a sparkling ice bridge and then pulled up high over a magnificent snowy valley. Tinker Bell's breath came in short puffs of frosty air. It was like nothing she had ever seen or felt before. No stories about the Winter Woods could have prepared her for this.

"I made it," she whispered to herself.

Up ahead, a handsome winter fairy flew over to greet her owl. Tinker Bell ducked down inside the basket, hiding.

"Welcome back," the winter fairy said to the owl. "You ready for the drop-off?"

The owl gave a nervous hoot.

"Come on," the winter fairy teased. "You did it yesterday. You'll be fine."

As Tinker Bell watched, the winter fairy flew ahead and spiraled down to a hilltop covered in snow. She realized that the owls were going to drop the baskets onto a long icy slide that would take them to a factory similar to the basket depot back in Tinkers' Nook. Tink gulped. This was going to be a bumpy ride!

On the winter fairy's signal, the owls swooped forward one by one and let go of their baskets. Tinker Bell's basket lurched to one side as her owl got ready to release it. Tink was thrown against the edge, and she accidentally hit the snowflake release lever!

Instantly, the trapdoor at the bottom of her basket sprang open. Her satchel started to slide toward it. Quickly, Tinker Bell snatched it up. But the basket rocked to and fro. She started to roll toward the open trapdoor herself!

Tink grabbed the edge of the opening just before she would have fallen through, and with all her strength, pulled herself back up and closed the trapdoor. *Whew!*

But Tink wasn't out of trouble yet. Her owl had been thrown off balance by her tumbling. Startled, he accidentally released the basket too soon. It careened out of control.

A winter fairy below spotted the renegade basket. "Look out!" he cried.

Tinker Bell's basket slid down the chute and smashed into a pile of bins already loaded with snowflakes. Frosty crystals flew everywhere! As her basket rolled to a stop, Tinker Bell remained perfectly still. The winter fairies were scampering to clean up the mess. Thankfully, no one had spotted her. Tink quickly started to gather all the things that had fallen out of her satchel. But wait—something was missing.

Tinker Bell peeked around the rim of her basket. The wing book was lying out in the open!

Just then, a large shadow passed overhead. A massive snowy owl whooshed by, and a powerful-looking fairy wearing a cape leapt down to the ground.

"Lord Milori," she heard the winter fairy in charge of the owls say. Tinker Bell gasped. That must be the Lord of Winter Fawn had told her about. The one who had made the rule that fairies couldn't cross the border. Now Tink really needed to stay hidden!

"And what happened here?" the lord asked in a deep but quiet voice.

"Bit of a bumpy landing," the winter fairy said, nodding to the young snowy owl. "It's only his second drop-off."

The owl gave the lord a sheepish grin.

"As long as the basket made it," Lord Milori said, his voice kind, "I'd say he did just fine." He looked around at the work the fairies were doing. "The snowflakes are looking quite beautiful."

As the fairies were talking, Tinker Bell tried to reach the wing book with her foot. But it was too far away. She stretched just a little bit more . . . and accidentally knocked the book with her toe. It slid out of reach, and right into Lord Milori's boot!

"Hmm," Lord Milori said, picking up the book. "Now, that is odd."

Tinker Bell smacked her hand against her head. This was a disaster!

Lord Milori studied the book carefully. After a long moment, he finally said, "It must have been left in the basket by accident." He handed the book to the winter fairy in charge. "Return this to the Keeper."

Tinker Bell breathed in sharply. *The Keeper!*

Lord Milori remained several minutes longer, admiring the work of the snowflake fairies. Then he mounted his owl and took off into the sky. Once he had left, the winter fairy picked up the book and headed out of the snowflake depot.

Tinker Bell watched him go. If he was off to see the Keeper, then there was only one thing to do. She was going to follow him!

Seven

In the Hall of Winter, just outside the Keeper's chamber doors, Tinker Bell listened carefully. She had followed the winter fairy all the way there, and he was speaking with the Keeper now.

"It came from the warm side, in one of the baskets," she heard him say. Then he turned to fly off. "Have a good day!" he called back to the Keeper.

Once the fairy was out of sight, Tinker Bell quietly stepped inside the chamber. But the floor was slippery. It was made entirely of ice. Tinker Bell could barely stand up.

She clung to a wall and struggled to get her balance. As she steadied herself, she noticed a soft purring noise coming from behind her. Slowly, she turned around. . . .

An enormous snowy lynx was just inches from her face! Tinker Bell clapped her hand over her mouth. But when the creature snored, she realized it was asleep. Sighing with relief, Tinker Bell backed away . . .

. . . and slipped on the ice! *"Ahhh!"* she cried as she slid down into the frozen depths of the hall. She kept sliding and sliding, until finally she crashed into a large stack of ice books against the wall. She breathed heavily for a moment. This was not going as well as she'd hoped. She staggered to her feet and looked around.

What she saw took her breath away. She was in a grand library, bigger than any room she had ever seen. Thousands of books lined the walls, and stacks of frosty parchments towered in every corner. Several large ice tablets teetered on the edges of their shelves, held in place by even more books and papers piled on top. It was incredible!

Across the room, Tinker Bell spotted the wing book that

the winter fairy had dropped off. She began to inch over to it when suddenly a short, elderly fairy walked in. He had tousled white hair and small, round spectacles. Tink could hear him mumbling to himself.

"Ah, that's the end of that chapter," the fairy was saying. "Boy, that's a beauty. *Flora and Fauna of the Fairies.*" He chuckled.

That must be the Keeper, Tinker Bell thought. She couldn't believe it. She had found him! She was just about to step out from behind the ice books when a young winter fairy came whizzing by.

"Keeper! Keeper!" the winter fairy shouted. Her voice was filled with urgency.

"Yes?" the Keeper answered, turning around.

"The most amazing thing happened!" the fairy gushed. "Yesterday, at the border. You'll never believe it!"

Tinker Bell watched as the fairy paused to catch her breath. The commotion had woken the snowy lynx from its nap, and it wandered into the room. "Hi, Fiona," the young winter fairy said to the large cat.

Then she turned back to the Keeper. "You've got to tell me what it means! Okay, my wings . . ."

As Tinker Bell listened, a tingling sensation suddenly overwhelmed her. She looked over her shoulder and saw that her wings were shimmering so brightly she could see them right through her coat.

"My wings, they actually . . . they lit up!" the young winter fairy finished. She gasped. "It's happening again!" She turned so that the Keeper could see that her wings were sparkling.

"Oooh," the Keeper said, amazed.

Tinker Bell peeked out from her hiding place and got a good look at the winter fairy's face for the first time. Her stomach did a little flip. Something felt so familiar about the fairy! She had short, silvery hair and ice-blue eyes. Her dress was made from a delicate material that glistened like frost in the sunlight. Tink was positive that she had never met this fairy. But she couldn't help feeling drawn to her. She took off her coat and stepped out of hiding.

The winter fairy turned and stared at Tinker Bell. They began drifting toward one another, as if they were guided by an invisible force.

"In all my years . . . ," the Keeper said quietly.

"Your wings," the winter fairy whispered. "They're sparkling."

"Like yours," Tinker Bell replied.

Then, as suddenly as it had started, the sparkling faded.

"Keeper?" the winter fairy asked.

"I've only heard of this," the Keeper said in amazement. "But I've never seen it right here in front of my own eyes." Then he chuckled excitedly. *"Ooh hoo hoo!"* His expression said that he knew more than either of the young fairies did about the sparkling. He rubbed his hands together, delighted. "Follow me!"

53

Eight

Quickly, the Keeper ushered Tinker Bell and the winter fairy through the vast hall. He pointed his cane toward a great room with a giant snowflake pattern on the floor.

The Keeper motioned for both fairies to stand in the center of the snowflake. "Your wings are safe in here," he assured Tinker Bell.

Tink placed her coat on top of his cane and flew with the winter fairy to the middle of the snowflake. The Keeper tapped his cane on the floor, and the room went dark. Instantly, the snowflake Tink and the winter fairy were standing on lit up and rose off the ground. Amazed, the two fairies held perfectly still.

"Just put your wings into the light," the Keeper instructed.

Together, the fairies lifted their wings into the sunlight streaming down from an opening in the ceiling. The rays shone through their wings. Then an incredible thing happened. The light began projecting images from their pasts on the icy chamber walls. The first picture was of Big Ben, the clock tower in London.

"The mainland," Tinker Bell whispered, recognizing the landmark.

The scene switched to a baby laughing for the first time. The fairies watched as the laugh split in two and landed on a dandelion. Two wisps from the flower took flight and danced across a night sky. They floated past the Second Star to the Right and headed straight toward Never Land! But before they could reach the Pixie Dust Tree, one got caught on a branch. The other traveled on. A strong gust of wind came and blew the tangled wisp in the opposite direction, toward the Winter Woods.

"Oh, no," Tink whispered.

Images of both fairies arriving in Pixie Hollow appeared—Tinker Bell in the warm seasons at the base of the Pixie Dust Tree, and the other fairy in the center of the Winter Woods.

"Two fairies born of the same laugh," Tinker Bell said slowly. "So that means . . ."

"You're my . . . ," the winter fairy began.

"Sister," they said at the same time.

The Keeper nodded and gestured to the fairies' wings. "Yes, your wings are identical," he said. "That's why they sparkle."

Turning their backs to each other, Tink and the winter fairy lined up their wings. The Keeper was right—the patterns matched perfectly! A bright spark of light suddenly burst forth when their wings touched. It created a beam that shone all the way up to the ceiling.

The two fairies jumped back. "Jingles!" they both cried. What was that?

"Ah," the Keeper said. "Maybe you shouldn't do that."

Tink smiled. "I'm Tinker Bell," she said happily.

"I'm Periwinkle," her sister replied.

Tink thought back to how her wings had sparkled the first time she jumped into winter. "So, you must have been at the border?" she asked slowly.

Periwinkle nodded. "Yeah, I was hoping to see the animals cross."

"I guess I didn't see you," Tink replied.

"Me either," Periwinkle said, smiling. Then she looked down at the pom-poms on Tink's boots. With an excited squeal, she reached into her pocket and pulled out two identical pom-poms. "I usually just wear them at home." She grinned.

At that moment, a deep voice bellowed through the chamber. "Hello, Keeper. Are you in?"

"Yumpin' yetis!" the Keeper exclaimed, startled. "Lord Milori!"

Periwinkle panicked. "If he sees you, he'll send you back," she said to Tinker Bell.

"Don't a-worry," the Keeper whispered. "I'm gonna take care of this."

"Keeper?" Lord Milori called. "I need to speak with you. It's important."

Tink and Periwinkle crouched down on the large, hovering snowflake. As long as they stayed up there, Lord Milori wouldn't be able to see them from down below.

"I'll be right back," the Keeper promised. Then he flew down to see Lord Milori.

"I'm right here," the Keeper told the royal fairy.

"Did you receive the wing book?" Lord Milori asked.

"You know, once upon a time you'd stop by just to say hello and howdy-do," the Keeper said, shaking his head. He pretended to look hurt.

Lord Milori sighed. "I'm sorry," he replied sincerely. "Hello," he added.

"Howdy-do," the Keeper chirped.

"This book has me worried," Lord Milori continued. "What if a warm fairy brought it here?"

The Keeper chuckled. "Well, that might be nice, then, meeting a warm fairy," he said. "Especially one with such good taste in books."

"It's too cold," Lord Milori said sternly.

"Well, maybe if they were wearing a coat or, you know, one of them little sweater vests," the Keeper replied lightly. "They're nice."

The look that crossed Lord Milori's face made it clear that he was losing his patience. "I'll remind you, crossing the border is forbidden."

"There was a time when it wasn't," the Keeper responded, growing serious.

"The rule is there to keep the fairies safe," Lord Milori said. "That will never change. If a warm fairy comes here, you will send them back."

He stared long and hard at the Keeper, and the elderly fairy dropped his gaze. "Of course," the Keeper agreed softly.

Up above on the floating snowflake, Tinker Bell and Periwinkle exchanged a worried look. This didn't sound good.

"Thank you," Lord Milori said, turning to leave.

Once he was out of sight, the snowflake Tinker Bell and Periwinkle were on descended to the floor. The Keeper turned to Tinker Bell sadly. "Well," he said, "you heard Lord Milori. You must go back home." He paused and thought for a moment. "Of course, he didn't say *when*," he added with a twinkle in his eye.

The sisters hugged and cheered, happy to have more time to spend together.

"Now, listen, you two," the Keeper told them. "It gets colder after dark, so it's best to get Tinker Bell home before the first moonlight."

Periwinkle gave the Keeper a big hug. "Thank you, Dewey," she said.

Tinker Bell glanced at her sister, confused. "Dewey?" she asked. What did that mean?

"That's his real name," Periwinkle explained.

"It's what my friends call me," said the Keeper.

A big smile spread across Tinker Bell's face. "Thank you, Dewey," she said happily.

Nine

The Winter Woods seemed even more spectacular to Tinker Bell now that her sister was showing her around. Icicles covered everything, and the pure-white snow sparkled on trees and in fields. To Tinker Bell, it appeared as if the whole world was glowing!

Together, the sisters visited Periwinkle's favorite spots. First they stopped at the Winter Field, with its endless mounds of snow that were perfect for sledding. Then they visited the Icicle Cave, with its hundreds of twinkling icicles in all shapes and sizes. Periwinkle flitted between frosted trees while Tink ran through snowdrifts. They even went to see the Pixie Dust Well. It was similar to the Pixie Dust Tree on the warm side of Pixie Hollow, except that the pixie dust here flowed from a hollow root. The root connected, underground, all the way back to the main Pixie Dust Tree on the warm side. This was where Periwinkle had arrived when she was born. Tinker Bell smiled. She would have loved to have been with her sister when they both arrived in Never Land.

But most of all, Tinker Bell and Periwinkle couldn't stop talking. There was so much to catch up on. They shared stories of their adventures. Periwinkle wanted to hear all about tinkering. And Tink listened with wide eyes as Periwinkle explained that she was a frost talent. It was her job to frost things throughout the Winter Woods.

Soon they reached Periwinkle's home. Tink had never seen anything like it. It was a cold but cozy cave nestled high up on the side of a snowy mountain. It even had an ice-crest ledge for a front porch. From the tip of the ledge, Tink could see all the way to the border of winter!

Periwinkle showed Tink her room, and opened a

drawer full of lost objects that she had collected. Tinker Bell pulled a paper clip from the treasures.

"You collect Lost Things, too?" she asked eagerly.

Periwinkle grinned. "I call them *Found* Things," she told Tink.

A short while later, the two sisters went ice-skating using skates they had made from the paper clips! Tink wasn't very steady on her feet, but Periwinkle was patient and helped her sister glide across the frozen pond. Later, they tried snowboarding . . . and wound up landing in a heap among the trees.

When the two fairies grew tired, they sat on a branch to rest. Down below, a snowflake fairy was busy twirling a handful of snow high in the air as if it were a pizza. Then she expertly poked out a pattern in the frosty crystals. Each flake she made floated gently past Tinker Bell and Periwinkle, and no two were alike.

Tinker Bell sighed. This was the best day ever!

It's time for the animals to cross the border
into the Winter Woods.

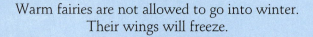

Warm fairies are not allowed to go into winter.
Their wings will freeze.

Tink crosses the border anyway.
Her wings begin to sparkle!

Tink finds a book about wings. She wants to talk
to the author, who lives in the Winter Woods.

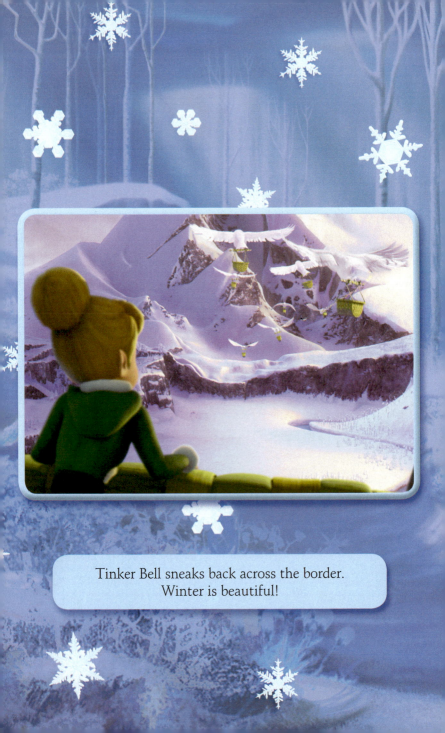

Tinker Bell sneaks back across the border.
Winter is beautiful!

Tink meets a frost fairy named Periwinkle.
They spend a day in the Winter Woods.

With the help of a snow machine, Periwinkle
can visit the warm side of Pixie Hollow.

Vidia, Silvermist, Rosetta, Iridessa, and Fawn can't wait to meet Periwinkle.

Periwinkle's wings get too warm.

Lord Milori forbids Tink and Peri
to see one another.

The seasons are out of balance. A freeze is coming!

Tink asks the winter fairies to protect
the Pixie Dust Tree with their frost.

Will the Pixie Dust Tree survive the freeze?

In the afternoon, Periwinkle took Tinker Bell to see two of her close friends in the Frost Forest. "That's Gliss," Periwinkle whispered, pointing to a fairy a short distance away. The two sisters didn't want to get caught, so they were hiding behind a snowy branch where the other fairies couldn't see them.

"And that's Spike," Periwinkle added.

Just then, Tinker Bell slipped and fell onto a snowdrift below. Periwinkle flew to catch her, and they both wound up sliding right into Gliss's and Spike's arms!

"Hi," Periwinkle said, smiling sheepishly at her friends.

When the two sisters had explained everything, Spike and Gliss looked at them in disbelief. "Sisters?" Spike asked, her eyebrows raised.

"Well, I think it's fantastic!" Gliss exclaimed. "You two look exactly alike! I mean, except for your clothes, and your hair, and Peri's a bit more pale." She took a deep breath and stood back to examine the two fairies.

"But your noses are *very* similar!" she said, nodding.

Spike shook her head. "Forget their noses. She's a warm fairy in winter!" She pointed at Tink.

"You're right!" Gliss agreed. "We gotta show her around." She smiled at Tinker Bell. "Oh, oh, oh! Let's take her ice-sliding."

Periwinkle turned to her sister with a knowing twinkle in her eye. "You are going to love this," she said.

Soon, all four fairies were teetering at the top of a high frozen waterfall aboard a toboggan.

"Ready, set, slide!" Periwinkle called out.

Tink shrieked in delight as they went racing down the icy hill. She couldn't remember ever having this much fun in her life.

That night, as the stars twinkled overhead, Periwinkle and Tinker Bell sat by a small campfire on the ice crest in front of Peri's home. They chatted quietly in the frosty night air.

"Favorite star?" Tinker Bell asked.

"Second Star—" Periwinkle started to say.

"—to the Right," Tink finished.

They laughed.

"Okay," Periwinkle said. "Favorite drink?"

"Hot chamomile tea," Tinker Bell said.

"Iced chamomile tea." Periwinkle giggled. She and her sister had so much in common!

"Okay, my turn," Tinker Bell said eagerly. She had the perfect question. "Favorite bug?"

"Bug?" Periwinkle paused for a moment. "It's too cold for bugs over here. But in one of Dewey's books I read about butterflies."

"Oh, in Butterfly Cove there are hundreds of them," Tinker Bell said. She looked out toward where she thought the center of Pixie Hollow would be. "It's in summer, right over . . ." She scanned the horizon, but all she could see was the frozen land of winter. "Hmm. I guess you can't see it from here."

"No, you can't," Periwinkle said sadly. She was quiet for a moment. Then she asked, "What's it like over there?"

"Warm," Tinker Bell answered.

"And the colors? The sounds? All the animals?" Periwinkle's eyes searched her sister's face. "And the fish! They swim in melted ice, right?"

Tinker Bell smiled. "Water," she said.

Periwinkle sighed. "I wish I could go there."

The two fairies sat side by side, watching the night sky. Then Tinker Bell looked at the tiny campfire that was keeping her comfortably warm. It gave her an idea.

"Peri?" she said slowly. "I made it warmer over here. Maybe I could make it colder over there."

Periwinkle gasped. "Are you saying *I* could cross?" The winter fairy's heart leapt. Crossing the border was something she had never thought was possible.

"Yeah!" Tinker Bell replied.

"Oh, Tink! You could show me your world. I could meet

your friends. Wait . . . do you think I could see a butterfly?" Periwinkle asked excitedly.

Tinker Bell smiled at her sister. "There's a pretty good chance," she said. Her mind was racing with ideas about how she could bring Periwinkle over to the warmer seasons. This would be her biggest tinkering challenge yet!

The two sisters were so busy chattering about their plans that they didn't notice that the campfire they had made was slowly melting the ice. It wasn't until they heard a loud *crack* that they realized something was very wrong.

Ten

The ice crest underneath them was collapsing!

Periwinkle quickly fluttered into the air. But Tinker Bell's wings were trapped beneath her coat. She panicked. "I can't fly!" she called out.

"Tink!" Periwinkle shouted. The frost fairy reached out to rescue Tinker Bell, but her sister's weight was too much for her.

"Hold on!" Periwinkle yelled, her voice strained. "Hold on!"

"I'm slipping!" Tinker Bell cried.

Periwinkle lost her grip on Tinker Bell, and they both screamed as they tumbled down through the ice and snow. Then, out of nowhere, Fiona the lynx appeared beneath them. The sisters landed on her back with a soft thump, and the lynx skillfully dodged the avalanche just in time. She carried the two fairies to safety.

"That's it, Fiona," Dewey said as he came flying up. "That's it." He turned to Tinker Bell and Periwinkle. "Are you girls all right?"

"Yeah," the sisters answered, out of breath. They couldn't stop shaking.

"Nothing broken? Nothing bruised?" Dewey asked.

Periwinkle shook her head. "No, we're okay."

Dewey dusted the snow from Tinker Bell's coat. His expression was serious. "Yeah, *this* time. Oh, Lord Milori was right," he said quietly. "Crossing the border is just too dangerous."

"Wh-what are you saying?" Tink asked anxiously.

"I'm sorry, girls. But I'm afraid this isn't going to work out like you hoped. We have to take Tinker Bell home."

Tinker Bell and Periwinkle looked at Dewey, stunned.

"It's . . . it's for your own good," Dewey said, his voice cracking.

The sisters tried to protest. But it was no use. They had to follow him to the border.

Fiona led the way, with Tink and Periwinkle riding on her back. The sisters held hands as the lynx brought them to the border. When they reached the edge, the two fairies remained quiet for a moment. They watched the soft snow curtain falling between autumn and winter.

Tink looked sadly at her sister. She gently pulled her hand away and began to walk back over the border.

"Oh, Tink," Periwinkle cried with tears in her eyes. She rushed to embrace her sister before she could cross.

"I can't watch, Fiona!" Dewey sniffled and turned to face the other way. "Such a shame. They're so cute together. It's for the best, though. At least they had today. I'm sure they'll both find happiness. Somehow."

Tinker Bell peeked over Periwinkle's shoulder to make

sure Dewey wasn't paying attention. Then she whispered in her sister's ear. "Okay, meet me here tomorrow," she said.

"Wh-what?" Periwinkle whispered back, surprised. "But we—"

Tinker Bell interrupted her. "I just met my long-lost sister for the first time, now you think I'm going to say good-bye forever?" She shook her head. "I don't think so!"

Periwinkle sighed in relief. "You really had me going there."

Tink smiled. "So, tomorrow," she said, "there's something I need you to bring. . . ."

Periwinkle nodded as Tink whispered her plan. Whatever her sister needed, she would get it. She wasn't going to let her down!

Eleven

Back on the warm side of Pixie Hollow, Tinker Bell knocked on Clank and Bobble's door. There were sounds of scuffling inside, followed by the door slowly opening. Tinker Bell peered around the edge.

"Guys?" she asked.

Foomp!

A net suddenly shot out and wrapped around her.

"Aagh!" Tinker Bell cried.

Clank stepped out with his spring-loaded troll-stopping gun in hand. A look of surprise crossed his face when he saw Tinker Bell trapped in the net.

"Tink! You're back!" Bobble gasped behind him.

"Yes," Tinker Bell said, slightly annoyed by the

unexpected greeting. She wriggled against the net.

"Sorry." Clank helped her get untangled. "We thought you were a troll."

"I knew we shouldn't have used the troll stopper." Bobble shook his head.

"But what if it *was* a troll?" Clank asked.

"Guys," Tinker Bell interrupted. "I need your help. But it's kind of a secret. I don't want everybody to know."

Tinker Bell's friends exchanged a glance. Then they looked at her with interest. When Tinker Bell had a secret plan in mind, they knew something exciting was about to start.

Tink quickly explained to Clank and Bobble about everything that had happened. Then she told them about her plan to bring Periwinkle to the warm side of Pixie Hollow. Soon, all three tinker fairies were busy at work. Tinker Bell and Bobble hammered away at a mysterious-looking contraption, while Clank went to collect extra Lost Things for them to use.

"Now, where is that Clanky?" Bobble asked after some time had passed.

"I'm right here," Clank replied, wheeling in a cart of extra supplies. Tinker Bell looked up to see what he had brought . . . and instead saw Fawn, Rosetta, Silvermist, Iridessa, and Vidia standing next to him.

"Oh," she sighed, feeling as if she had been caught.

"I didn't tell *everybody*," Clank assured her. "Just Fawn, Ro, Sil, Dess, and Vidia."

Vidia flew right in Tinker Bell's face and looked her up and down. She crossed her arms. "So, there's another you?" she asked matter-of-factly.

"Vidia!" Rosetta scolded.

Tinker Bell nodded. "Yeah, I've got a sister."

"I told you," Clank said proudly.

Tinker Bell told her fairy friends all about the Winter

Woods, and how she and Periwinkle had been born of the same laugh. She explained how Periwinkle's wings were identical to hers, and how both sisters' wings sparkled when they were near one another.

"I'm making this machine so she can come here and meet you all," Tinker Bell said. "And after that, we'll go straight to Queen Clarion."

Tink's friends exchanged worried glances.

"Um, have you thought this through?" Vidia asked.

"When Queen Clarion hears how we found each other, and that we're sisters, she'll change Lord Milori's rule," Tinker Bell said determinedly.

"Of course she will," Rosetta said.

"It's like you found the perfect Lost Thing," Silvermist said with a smile.

"And I'm never going to lose her," Tinker Bell replied.

"Well, then let's get to work!" Iridessa exclaimed.

Tinker Bell clapped her hands and grinned from ear to

ear. She was so happy that her friends were going to help her with her plan. With everyone working together, she just knew everything would turn out perfectly. She had the best friends in Pixie Hollow!

And soon her friends would see that she had the best sister in Pixie Hollow, too.

Twelve

All was silent at the border between autumn and winter. Not a single fairy was in sight. Quietly, a rust-colored leaf from autumn and a large snowflake from winter drifted closer to the dividing line. Then the leaf and the snowflake began to glow. It was Tinker Bell and Periwinkle!

"Anyone see you?" Tinker Bell asked, peeking out from under her leaf.

"No, you?" Periwinkle whispered back.

"Nope," said Tinker Bell.

The two girls sighed in relief and tossed aside their disguises.

"Did you bring it?" Tinker Bell asked.

"Yes," Periwinkle answered. She turned back to the

Winter Woods and whistled. A moment later, Periwinkle's friends Gliss, Sled, Spike, and Slush came out of hiding. They were holding ropes that were tied securely around a huge block of ice.

"For the record," Spike said, tugging at the rope, "we shouldn't be doing this. Whatever it is we're doing."

But the other fairies seemed more cheerful. They set the heavy block of ice down on the log bridge that connected the two seasons.

"As ordered. One big block of ice!" Sled announced.

Tinker Bell smiled. Then she turned and whistled. A moment later, Clank and Bobble rolled out a large contraption on wheels. It was covered with tubes, pulleys, ropes, and spinning fans.

"Ooooh," Gliss said, her eyes wide. "It's . . . uh . . . it's one of those . . ."

Spike leaned over to Periwinkle. ". . . things we shouldn't be doing," she whispered.

Clank and Bobble popped out from behind the giant invention. "It's a snowmaker!" Bobble exclaimed.

"It makes snooooooow!" Clank cried, waving his hands in the air for emphasis.

"This is your ticket to the warm side of Pixie Hollow," Tinker Bell said to Periwinkle with a satisfied grin.

Periwinkle couldn't believe it. She was actually going to be able to travel to the warm seasons! She took a step forward but then felt Spike pull her back.

"Wait a second," Spike said. "This is crazy. You don't even know if this thing works!"

"Oh, it works, all right," Clank chimed in.

Bobble pushed his goggles up. "Aye, we made it ourselves!" he said proudly.

Periwinkle moved closer to the machine, but was careful not to cross the border just yet. "How does it work?" she asked curiously.

Tinker Bell gave the signal and Clank moved a lever on

the cart. In a flash, a large claw on the back of the snowmaker lifted the cube of ice. Clank reeled the ice in, and a sharp grater on the machine began shaving off thin chips from the block. Soon, snowflakes began pouring out of a tube at the top.

"Wow!" Sled whispered, amazed.

Periwinkle beamed with pride. "You did it," she said to her sister. "You actually did it!"

Cautiously, Periwinkle flew over the border and into the column of snow. She looked unsteady for a moment. But then the cold flakes from the snowmaker swirled around her, making her feel right at home.

"Wow," she gasped. It was as cold as winter, even though she was on the other side of the border.

Clank adjusted a few levers on the snowmaker. "All righty," he said excitedly. "Your tour begins with the Autumn Forest. Then it's a quick stop in Springtime Square. And finally, the Pixie Dust Tree! Which, as you know, makes all fairy life possible."

"Aye, that's where you'll be meeting Her Majestyness, the queen," Bobble added.

"The queen?" Periwinkle asked in surprise.

Gliss's eyes widened. She nudged her friends. "They're going to see the queen!"

Tinker Bell hadn't told Periwinkle about this part of the plan. The frost fairy glanced nervously at Tink.

"She's very wise," Tink assured her. "And if we tell her we're sisters, she'll change Lord Milori's rule."

"That is so exciting!" Gliss blurted out. "Say hi for me, or do a curtsy, or whatever it is you do!"

"Sure!" Periwinkle laughed.

"And bring me back an acorn!" Gliss called. She held out her arms wide. "A *big* one!"

Tinker Bell made a grand, sweeping gesture with her hand. "After you," she said.

"Bye!" Periwinkle called to her friends. And she headed off with Tink, Clank, and Bobble into the Autumn Forest.

As the friends left, no one noticed the large, snowy owl watching them from high above on a tree branch. The owl waited until the fairies had disappeared. Then with a soft hoot, it quickly took flight to warn Lord Milori of what it had witnessed.

Thirteen

Periwinkle was amazed by the warm side of Pixie Hollow. Everything was so different than in the Winter Woods. So lively! Plants grew tall, and trees were covered with thick green leaves. Animals of all shapes, sizes, and colors scampered about. But the best part was seeing the fish. They really did swim in melted ice!

Clank and Bobble kept the snowmaker cranking a steady stream of snowflakes over Periwinkle everywhere she went—even while she floated down the river on a lily pad. As they drifted down the stream, Tinker Bell glanced up at the tree branches overhead. Silvermist, Rosetta, Fawn, Iridessa, and Vidia were hiding there. She winked, giving them the signal. It was time to show her sister what the warm-weather fairies could *really* do.

Silvermist went first. She dipped her hand in the stream and created a water arc above the sisters' heads. When Periwinkle looked up, she was delighted to see fish swimming in a bubble of water right over her.

Rosetta was up next. She flew ahead of Tinker Bell and Periwinkle and made an entire field of flowers burst into bloom. Periwinkle gasped when she saw all the colors. Then Tinker Bell motioned to Fawn. At a signal from the animal fairy, hundreds of butterflies filled the air.

"Butterflies!" Periwinkle exclaimed.

"Surprise!" Tink's friends cried, all flying down at once.

"Your friends did all this?" Periwinkle asked.

"They wanted to surprise you," Tinker Bell explained proudly. "Everyone, this is Periwinkle, my sister."

"This is so exciting," Silvermist said, clapping her hands together.

Then Rosetta stepped forward. "Hello," she said in a

loud, slow voice, as though Periwinkle wouldn't understand her language. "It—is—nice—to—meet—you. I—am—Rosetta. This—is . . ."

Vidia rolled her eyes. "Ro, she's a winter fairy. She's not from the moon."

"Oh, right," Rosetta said, embarrassed. Her cheeks flushed. "I'm just so excited."

Periwinkle smiled. "It's great to meet all of you."

Silvermist flew in closer. "This is so remarkable!" She looked back and forth between Tinker Bell and Periwinkle. "You two *are* sisters!"

Vidia put her arm around Periwinkle. "A little fairy-to-fairy advice," she whispered. "Tink can be a bit tricky to get along with at times."

"Yeah," Tinker Bell said sarcastically. "Look who's talking."

"We can't believe you're over here," Fawn chimed in, changing the subject.

"So are you cold enough?" Iridessa asked.

Periwinkle did a little spin inside her cone of snow. "It's perfect," she said.

"Oh, I nearly forgot!" Rosetta exclaimed. "This is for you. It's called a periwinkle also." She handed the winter fairy a delicate blue flower.

"Thank you. I'll keep it forever." Periwinkle said. She waved her hand across the flower, and instantly it was encased in a thin layer of frost.

The warm-weather fairies were amazed.

"It's frost," Tinker Bell explained. "She and her friends practice in the Frost Forest. You should see it."

The fairies continued chattering excitedly. They couldn't believe Tinker Bell actually had a sister! But as they talked, they didn't notice Periwinkle's wings slowly beginning to droop.

Suddenly, the frost fairy sank to the ground. "I don't feel so . . . ," she said weakly.

"Periwinkle!" Tinker Bell cried. She rushed to her sister's side.

"My wings," Periwinkle whispered, frightened. The frost fairy's wings were beginning to wilt! "I can't feel them. I think they're too warm."

Bobble looked up at the snowmaker. He was pedaling quickly to keep the snow coming. But he realized that the snowflakes were starting to dwindle.

"It's running out of ice!" Clank exclaimed.

"We have to get her back to the border," Fawn declared.

Periwinkle gazed up at Tinker Bell. "What about the queen?" she said in a small voice.

"There's no time," Tinker Bell exclaimed. She turned to Clank and Bobble. "Clank, grab some ice. We'll wrap her wings."

Everyone sprang into action, scraping up fallen snow to surround Peri's drooping wings. Together, they all pushed the snowmaker toward the border.

"Come on," Iridessa cried. "We can do this!"

Bobble pedaled as fast as his legs could go.

"We're almost there," Tinker Bell called out. She turned to Periwinkle. "Not much farther," she said. But her heart sank when she saw the strained look on Periwinkle's face. They were running out of time.

Just as the machine used up the last bit of ice and the snowflakes stopped coming, Tinker Bell and Vidia tumbled with Periwinkle back across the border. The winter fairy fell to the ground the minute they crossed the bridge. She was too weak to even stand.

Tinker Bell helped unwrap her sister's wings. When the snow fell away, Tink's hand flew to her mouth. Instead of being iridescent and sparkling, Periwinkle's wings were brown and wilted.

Just then, the fairies caught sight of Lord Milori. He swooped down on his snowy owl and hurried toward the injured frost fairy.

"Please," Tinker Bell begged, "can you help her?"

"Tink," Vidia said urgently. It was getting too cold for them. Vidia quickly pulled Tinker Bell back across the border to safety.

On the winter side, Lord Milori knelt down beside Periwinkle and placed his hands on her shoulders. His face was filled with concern. "Gently," he said in a soft voice. "Lift your wings. Let the cold surround them."

Slowly, Periwinkle raised her wings. Little by little, as the cold air swirled around her, Peri's wings began to regain their shimmer and color. She tried to flutter them, and sighed with relief when they worked.

"You're okay." Tinker Bell exhaled, leaning back against Vidia. "Your wings are okay."

"This is why we do not cross the border," Lord Milori said quietly.

"No, it could have worked!" Periwinkle protested. "We just needed a bigger piece of ice."

Lord Milori shook his head sadly. "And when that was gone?" he asked.

Periwinkle started to reply, but then realized she didn't know what to say.

"Your wings could have broken," the Lord of Winter continued.

"But they didn't," Periwinkle replied. "I'm fine." She pointed to Tinker Bell and her friends on the other side of the bridge. "Thanks to them."

Lord Milori looked at Tinker Bell and the other warm-weather fairies. His expression grew harder. "The rule is there to protect you," he said to Tink and Peri. "I'm sorry. You two may never see each other again." He stood to leave.

"Please don't do this," Periwinkle begged. "We belong together."

"We're sisters!" Tinker Bell shouted. "We were born of the same laugh."

At this, Lord Milori paused. Then he looked back. "All

the more reason you should want to keep each other safe," he said.

A tear escaped from Periwinkle's eye. How could the best day of her life be ending so horribly?

"Come on, Tink," Vidia urged. "Let's go home."

But Tinker Bell felt angry and hurt. She glared at Lord Milori. "No! Lord Milori, your rule will not keep us apart!" she shouted forcefully.

"Tinker Bell, this is not Lord Milori's rule," a voice suddenly said behind them. Tink turned to see Queen Clarion standing a short distance away. "It's mine."

"Queen Clarion?" Tinker Bell asked. She couldn't believe that her own queen was keeping her from her sister.

"I'm sorry," the queen replied.

Tinker Bell and Periwinkle looked at one another across the border. Their plan to be together was falling apart.

"You should get deeper into the cold," Lord Milori instructed Periwinkle.

But Periwinkle couldn't bear it. She rushed to the edge of the border and threw her arms around her sister. They had been so happy together during the day, and now they weren't sure if they'd ever see each other again. Periwinkle squeezed her sister tight, and they hugged for a long while. Then Periwinkle flew away. Tinker Bell watched her go. With slumped shoulders, she followed her friends back into the Autumn Forest.

Queen Clarion and Lord Milori were left alone on the bridge. The queen looked up at him, and her eyes grew sad. She turned to fly away.

Without a word, Lord Milori mounted his owl and rose high into the air. But before he headed deeper into winter, he steered his owl to swoop down and knock the snowmaker off the bridge. The machine tumbled into the riverbed below. He wanted to be certain that no fairy would ever try such a dangerous stunt again.

His owl flapped its wings, and they flew off into the

cold. As Lord Milori disappeared over the horizon, he didn't see the machine land next to a waterfall at the bottom of the riverbed. One by one, large chunks of ice began to feed into the grater. And little by little, the ice turned into frosty snowflakes that quietly blew across the border and into the Autumn Forest.

Fourteen

The Keeper was in the Hall of Winter, trying hard to keep his focus. He was supposed to be writing, but he was distracted. He put down his pen and glanced at an open door a short distance away. Periwinkle had been inside that room for most of the day. He went over and poked his head in to check on her.

She was sitting in the middle of the large snowflake, mesmerized by the images projected on the icy walls. Again and again, she watched the story of how she and Tinker Bell had been born.

Just then, Lord Milori walked past Dewey and up to the edge of the snowflake. Periwinkle turned to him, her eyes filled with tears. The Keeper ducked out of the room. He hoped that Lord Milori would be able to comfort the young frost fairy.

At the same time, on the warm side of Pixie Hollow, Tinker Bell was with Queen Clarion in her chambers. She had begged the queen to reconsider her rule. The queen smiled sadly at Tinker Bell. "Long ago," she began, "when Pixie Hollow was very young, two fairies met and fell in love. One of them was a winter fairy."

In the Hall of Winter, Lord Milori was telling Periwinkle the same tale. "And the other was from the warm seasons," he said. "The two fairies were enchanted with each other, and every sunset they met at the border . . ."

". . . where spring touches winter," Queen Clarion continued. "But as their love grew stronger, they wished to be together."

"And share each other's worlds," Lord Milori said. "So they disregarded the danger and crossed."

"One of them broke a wing," Queen Clarion finished quietly. "For which there is no cure."

"From that day forward," said Lord Milori, "Queen Clarion declared that fairies must never again cross the border. And I agreed that our two worlds should forever remain apart."

Periwinkle wiped a tear from her cheek. "And the two fairies?" she said.

"What happened to them?" Tink asked Queen Clarion.

The queen's gaze fell. "They had to say good-bye," she whispered.

Tinker Bell's shoulders slumped. It was no use. She would never see her sister again. Quietly, she walked over to a large window in the queen's chambers. As she looked outside, she saw a tiny snowflake float down from the sky. She drew in a sharp breath.

Oh, no, she thought.

Fifteen

In a flash, Queen Clarion and Tinker Bell raced through the Autumn Forest. Other fairies followed, including Fawn, Rosetta, Iridessa, Silvermist, Vidia, and the seasons' ministers. Snowflakes were falling more rapidly now, and fairies throughout the warm seasons were panicking.

"The temperature seems to be plummeting!" the Minister of Autumn cried.

"The hibiscuses are halfway to hibernation!" added the Minister of Summer.

"Now, now, ministers," Queen Clarion said, trying to remain calm. "Let's not panic."

But as they reached the top of a steep hill near the border and looked into the distance, they gasped.

"Snow!" the Minister of Spring cried.

They couldn't believe their eyes. Snow was billowing up into the sky from the edge of the border, and it was beginning to blanket the warm seasons of Pixie Hollow!

Just then, Tinker Bell heard Clank and Bobble. They were struggling down below in the riverbed by the border. She flew toward the sound of their voices and found them on a ledge near an icy waterfall. They were trying to move the snowmaker.

"Heave ho!" the tinkers cried.

"What happened?" Tink asked when she reached her friends. She pointed to the machine. "How did this get here?" The last time she'd seen the snowmaker, it had been on the bridge.

"I don't know, Miss Bell." Clank shrugged. "But it's stuck real good."

"Aye," Bobble said. He pointed to the mound of snow

piling high into the sky. "And it's making that thing bigger by the minute!"

Tinker Bell called to Rosetta and the rest of her friends to help move the snowmaker. With all their might, the fairies pushed and shoved. Finally, the machine broke free. It tumbled deeper into the riverbed and splashed into the water.

"We did it!" the fairies cheered.

"It's over." Tinker Bell sighed.

"Uh . . . I don't think it is," Vidia said slowly. She pointed up at the sky.

Though the machine was gone, the snow was still coming down. A cold breeze ruffled the fairies' clothes and sent chills to the tips of their wings.

"Why isn't it stopping?" Clank asked.

Queen Clarion and the ministers all looked concerned. "It's too late," the queen said. "The seasons have been thrown out of balance."

"But if the temperature continues to drop, it will freeze all of Pixie Hollow," the Minister of Spring said.

All the fairies looked to Queen Clarion for guidance. But she remained silent. Just then, a sharp *crack* behind them grabbed their attention. The fairies watched as a large, frozen tree branch broke and fell to the ground.

The Minister of Autumn turned to the queen with a grave expression on his face. "Queen Clarion," he said. "The Pixie Dust Tree . . ."

The queen's eyes grew wide. Immediately, she flew high into the sky and gazed at the Pixie Dust Tree in the center of Pixie Hollow. Her face clouded with worry. "We must hope the tree survives," she said. "Otherwise there will be no more pixie dust." She paused. "Life in Pixie Hollow will change forever. And no fairy will ever fly again."

The fairies all gasped, picturing life without the Pixie Dust Tree.

The queen motioned to the fairies. "Hurry," she said. "We must do everything we can!"

✿ ✿ ✿

Everyone in Pixie Hollow began to prepare for the coming freeze. The fairies needed to make sure that they and all the animals would be able to stay warm until the cold had passed. Iridessa took an armful of fireflies and placed them in a sunflower, which Rosetta closed up around them. Over by Havendish Stream, Fawn escorted a group of frogs into an empty log and patted it closed with moss.

Meanwhile, Fairy Mary was directing the tinker fairies to pile moss onto the Pixie Dust Tree. "That's it," she instructed them. "Lay the blankets along the branches, as many as you can. We must protect the tree."

In her teapot home, Tinker Bell was helping several pillbugs keep cozy. "There you go," she said, lowering a pillbug onto her bed. "You guys just stay here and keep warm. Everything's going to be—"

Suddenly, a twinkle from the corner of the room caught Tinker Bell's eye. She turned to see Periwinkle's frosted blue flower resting on her table. Rosetta must have brought it to her house after they had taken Periwinkle back to the Winter Woods. Tink flew over to examine the flower. Part of the frost casing had broken away. She couldn't believe what she saw. The flower's petals stretched wide in full bloom.

"It's still alive!" Tink breathed.

Slowly, an idea began to form in her mind. If the frost had helped keep the flower alive, then maybe . . .

Tink looked out the window, in the direction of the Winter Woods.

"Peri," she whispered.

Sixteen

Periwinkle raced through the Winter Woods ahead of Dewey. The elderly fairy was doing his best to keep up with her, but the blustery wind was strong and made it difficult for him to fly.

"Dewey, you gotta see this!" Periwinkle called.

"I'm sure there's nothing to worry about!" Dewey assured her. But as they reached the place where Periwinkle was taking him, he stopped short. "Oh, dear," he said.

Periwinkle joined her friends Gliss and Spike at the edge of the Pixie Dust Well. Normally, there would be a steady stream of pixie dust flowing from the root above it. But there was no flow of pixie dust now. There was nothing— not even a trickle.

"There must be something wrong with the Pixie Dust Tree," Periwinkle said.

Dewey examined the hollow root and tapped his cane on it. One last speck of dust fell into his palm. He furrowed his brow. "Yeah, you might want to worry just a little bit," he said.

At that moment, Periwinkle's wings began sparkling.

"Tink?" she asked in shock. Periwinkle flew up and looked out over the white landscape. On the horizon, racing straight toward them, was Tinker Bell! She was carrying her winter coat so that her wings were exposed and she could fly. But they were quickly icing over.

"Periwinkle!" Tink shouted. She fought against the freezing gusts that whipped past her. There was no time to lose. Tink had to reach her sister. All of Pixie Hollow was counting on her! But the cold was just too strong. Before she could get there, Tinker Bell fell to the ground in a heap.

"Tinker Bell!" Periwinkle cried. She, Dewey, and

her friends rushed to where Tink had fallen.

Meanwhile, Tink lifted her head from the snow. Something was wrong. She looked back at her wings and gasped. They had turned ice blue! Quickly, she hid them under her coat so Periwinkle wouldn't see how cold they had become.

Periwinkle and her friends helped Tink sit up. "Are you okay?" Periwinkle asked, her face filled with concern. "Why would you *fly* here?"

"I had to," Tink panted. "Pixie Hollow's in trouble. There's a freeze, and the Pixie Dust Tree is in danger."

Dewey looked at the winter fairies. "That explains it," he said.

A terrible feeling formed in Periwinkle's stomach. "Our dust here . . . it already stopped flowing," she said.

Tink handed them the blue periwinkle flower she'd brought with her. "I think there's something you can do," she explained. "Your frost . . . it kept the flower alive."

Gliss stepped forward. "Frost does that. It's like a little blanket. It tucks the warm air inside and keeps out the cold."

Periwinkle's eyes grew wide. "We could frost the Pixie Dust Tree before the freeze hits it!"

Tinker Bell smiled. She had known that her sister would understand.

But Spike seemed doubtful. "What about our wings?"

Dewey shook his head. "If it's a freeze, it will be cold enough to cross."

The fairies all looked at one another.

"Then what are we waiting for?" Spike asked.

Seventeen

Minutes later, the fairies were flying back across the border. Fiona carried Tinker Bell, while the winter fairies zoomed overhead. As they passed through to the Autumn Forest, they all stared in shock.

"The freeze is moving so fast," Tinker Bell said, gazing at the frozen landscape. "We have to get to the tree."

Back in the center of Pixie Hollow, Queen Clarion, Clank, Bobble, Fairy Mary, and all the fairies were hard at work trying to protect the tree. They passed thick, mossy blankets to one another and carefully laid them along the branches. But for every blanket they put in place, the cold wind whipped another one off.

"It's not working," Clank called out anxiously to Fairy Mary.

109

"The wind is too strong!" Bobble added.

The queen's face was etched with worry. Suddenly, they heard a growl behind them. Everyone turned and watched in disbelief as Tink, Peri, Gliss, and Spike rode up to them on Fiona's back.

"Tinker Bell?" Queen Clarion cried in surprise when she saw her with the three frost fairies.

"Queen Clarion, they can help," Tink explained. "Their frost is like a blanket. It can protect the tree."

Queen Clarion studied Tinker Bell's face for a moment. Then she turned to Periwinkle, Gliss, and Spike. "Do it," she instructed them.

The warm-weather fairies all watched hopefully as Peri and her friends flitted from branch to branch and began frosting the tree as quickly as they could. But the freeze was advancing fast.

"We should hand out the rest of the blankets and use them to protect our wings," Tinker Bell called to Clank and Bobble.

They began distributing blankets to all the warm-weather fairies. One by one, everyone began hurrying inside the Pixie Dust Tree. It would be warm and safe in there until the freeze passed.

Meanwhile, up above, Periwinkle, Gliss, and Spike were growing tired.

"The tree is too big," Spike panted. She eyed the freeze line. It was getting closer by the minute. "We're never going to make it."

Just then, far off in the distance, an owl screeched. Everyone turned toward the sound. Lord Milori was flying in on his majestic snowy owl! Beside him, Dewey was perched on the back of the young owl that had first carried Tinker Bell into the Winter Woods.

And together, they were leading an entire squadron of winter fairies toward the Pixie Dust Tree! There were hundreds of them.

"Lord Milori!" Periwinkle cried in astonishment.

"We've come to help," the lord said in his deep voice when they landed.

Periwinkle quickly explained how they were frosting the tree to protect it, but that the tree was too large for them to cover on their own.

"Understood," Lord Milori replied. He faced the army of winter fairies. "Start at the freeze line and spread out to the other seasons," he commanded. "The rest of you, cover the tree!"

Instantly, the winter fairies sprang into action. Sled led a group to frost the meadows and fields while Lord Milori directed the fairies blanketing the Pixie Dust Tree from atop his owl. Soon, all of Pixie Hollow was a glittering landscape of frost. When the last branch was covered, Lord Milori swooped down to the ground.

"We've done all we can," he said to the frost fairies around the Pixie Dust Tree. He looked at Tink and her friends. "You must take cover."

The warm-weather fairies hurried inside the tree, out of the cold. But Queen Clarion remained outside a minute longer. She looked at Lord Milori and shivered. "Will everything be all right?" she asked.

Lord Milori gazed at the queen for a long time. "I don't know," he answered finally. "I've never seen anything like this."

Queen Clarion shivered again. Lord Milori took off his cloak and gently placed it around her shoulders. "Please take cover," he said to her.

Before she left, the queen stole one more glance at the Lord of Winter. When her old friend turned, she could see his broken right wing. The legend that she had told Tinker Bell was in fact the story of her love for Lord Milori. Without another word, she joined the others in the depths of the Pixie Dust Tree to wait for the freeze to arrive.

Eighteen

Lord Milori and the winter fairies stood watch as the freeze took hold of Pixie Hollow. Arctic winds swept across the glades, and icy cold enveloped the fairy world. Deep inside the Pixie Dust Tree, Tinker Bell and her friends huddled together for warmth. They couldn't see the frozen world outside, but they could hear the howling winds and feel the giant tree creaking and swaying around them.

Darkness spread throughout Never Land.

After a long, long while, Tinker Bell finally saw a beam of light shining in through a knothole in the tree. She peered out of her hiding place and gasped. Everything was covered in snow and ice! But the sun was shining brightly.

Cautiously, all the fairies began to emerge from the tree. Periwinkle flew over to join Tinker Bell, and one by one, the fairies moved toward the Pixie Dust Well. They gazed in silence at the frozen stream of pixie dust that had stopped in midflow over the pool. Everyone held their breath. Had their plan worked? Was the tree saved?

Very slowly, the sun began to melt the ice. The pixie dust began to flow!

Everyone burst into loud cheers. Some fairies wiped tears of joy from their eyes.

"What a beautiful sight," Bobble said, sniffling and wiping his goggles.

Periwinkle turned to her sister, and a wide grin broke over her face. "It worked, Tinker Bell!" she cried.

Fairies flew high into the air, celebrating. Periwinkle spun happily in a circle. They were safe. Their frost had saved Pixie Hollow!

Then Periwinkle looked down. Tinker Bell was still

standing on the branch below. "Tink?" Periwinkle asked. She flew down and landed beside her sister on the tree limb. "What's wrong?"

Tinker Bell smiled sadly at Periwinkle. Then she turned around so her sister could see her wings.

One of them was broken.

"Tinker Bell!" all her friends gasped.

"Oh, no," whispered Iridessa.

Periwinkle gazed at her sister. "When you fell in winter," she said, remembering how Tinker Bell had flown to get the winter fairies. "Why didn't you tell me?"

"We had to save the tree." Tinker Bell shrugged. "Besides, there's no cure for a broken wing."

Periwinkle hugged Tinker Bell tight. "I'm so sorry."

Lord Milori stepped forward. "This happened because we tried to keep you apart," he said quietly.

"But never again," Queen Clarion declared next to him. "You belong together."

Dewey was standing nearby. Tears began to form in his eyes as he watched the sisters.

Tinker Bell looked up. "It's getting warmer," she said, feeling the growing strength of the sun. "You should get back to winter."

But Periwinkle couldn't let go.

"Hey, I'll be okay," Tinker Bell said with a small smile. "I'll meet you tomorrow at the border. Sisters?"

"Sisters," Periwinkle replied. She put her wings up to Tinker Bell's, and gently, the swirling patterns in each of their wings began to glow.

Then something unexpected happened. A surge of energy rushed between their wings, like a spark. Quickly, the sisters stepped apart.

"Jingles!" they both cried.

But Tinker Bell felt a tingling in her broken wing. Both sisters watched in awe as a sparkling light began to dance around the torn edges. They looked at one another.

Then, with a deep breath, they turned wing to wing once more.

The moment they touched, the sisters' wings burst into a brilliant ball of energy! It was so bright that the two fairies had to shield their eyes from the glow. The light shone high into the sky, reflecting off the melting ice and snow. When the sparkling finally faded, everyone stared in awe.

Tinker Bell's wing was healed!

Before she could even hug her sister, Tink's friends bombarded her. They cheered and cried. Tinker Bell was safe—her sister had healed her!

Queen Clarion and Lord Milori watched happily. The Lord of Winter reached out, took the queen's hand, and gently kissed her.

Dewey smiled as the friends, old and new, rejoiced. He would have much more to write about in his books when he returned home.

Nineteen

A few days later, at the border of the Winter Woods, winter fairies took turns frosting warm-weather fairies' wings. Now that they knew the secret of how to cross over into the cold without getting hurt, the warm-weather fairies couldn't wait to get their first taste of winter!

Silvermist had just finished having her wings frosted. She thanked the two winter fairies, then flew across the border to join Fawn and Iridessa on the other side.

Next in line was Fairy Mary. She was very nervous. Though she was bundled up in warm clothing, she was still unsure about crossing over.

"Next!" the fairy organizing the line called impatiently.

Fairy Mary took a deep breath and lifted her wings

to be frosted. As the cold hit her, she squealed. Then a smile spread across her face. "Ooooh, that feels good," she said.

All over the Winter Woods, warm-weather fairies were discovering the beauty of winter. New friendships were also blooming. Rosetta was just admiring her reflection in a big block of ice when Sled flew up beside her. He had noticed her earlier and wanted to introduce himself.

"Hi," he said.

Rosetta blushed. "Hello," she replied.

"I'm Sled." He held out his hand.

"Oh my, that's perfect," Rosetta blurted out. Then her cheeks flushed with embarrassment. "Oh, I'm Rosetta," she added.

"Rosetta." Sled smiled. "That's beautiful." He took her hand, and together they went to join their friends by the skating pond.

Meanwhile, Clank and Bobble had a very special

delivery. "Oh, Misssss Glisssss!" Bobble called out excitedly.

Gliss had been standing near the skating pond, chatting with Spike and Vidia. When she turned around, her eyes grew wide. Clank and Bobble were carrying an enormous acorn!

"An acorn," she gasped.

"Biggest one we could find." Bobble grinned.

Gliss squealed with delight. "I love it!" She quickly flew over to examine the acorn from every angle.

Vidia turned to Spike with raised eyebrows. Spike shrugged. "She likes acorns," Spike explained.

"Must be a winter thing," Vidia replied.

Not far away, Queen Clarion and Lord Milori were gliding across the ice, hand in hand. After so many years of being apart, they were thrilled to be reunited.

And over by the border, Periwinkle was smiling as she watched the fairies cross over one by one. Suddenly, her wings began to sparkle. "Tink," she said.

Periwinkle flew to meet her sister as she entered the Winter Woods.

"You ready?" Tink asked.

"Ready." Periwinkle nodded.

At the same time, the sisters whistled. Instantly, a large flock of snowy owls burst into the sky. They released snowflakes and periwinkles from baskets they were carrying. All the fairies gazed up in wonder at the incredible sight.

Tink and Periwinkle smiled at one another. It was beautiful, but not nearly as magical as the secret of their wings. The two fairies had discovered that the bond of sisterhood was the greatest magic of all. And they knew they would never be apart again.